MW00874902

irresistible

irresistible

stranger

stranger

LUCIA FRANCO

Copyright © 2023 by Lucia Franco

Edited by Nadine Winningham
Cover Design by The Kat Savage Designs

All rights reserved. No part of this publication may be reproduced, distributed, or transmitted in any form or by any means, including photocopying, recording, or other electronic or mechanical methods, without the prior written permission of the publisher, except in the case of brief quotations embodied in critical reviews and certain other noncommercial uses permitted by copyright law.

This is a work of fiction. Names, characters, businesses, places, events and incidents are either the products of the author's imagination or used in a fictitious manner. Any resemblance to actual persons, living or dead, or actual events is purely coincidental.

All Rights Reserved.

Also by Lucia Franco

Standalone Titles

You'll Think of Me

Hold On to Me

Hush Hush

Say Yes

You're Mine Tonight

Tell Me What You Want

Off Balances Series

Balance

Execution

Release

Twist

Dismount

Out of Bounds

LEO + TRISTA

The stranger sitting to my left hasn't taken his eyes off me since I walked into the bar.

He buys me a drink, and I tell him why I'm nursing my self-esteem. He's relentless in his pursuit. It's just the kind of attention a girl needs after two bad breakups when my ex walks in.

The same ex who told me he wanted to explore the ocean after I gave him three years of my life.

The man says he'll play the part of my fake boyfriend if I stay with him for the night. He promises to put on a good show for the ex and set the bar for the next man who visits my bed.

So I take him up on his offer.

CHAPTER ONE
TRISTA

The driver drops me off at the only bar in the city that permits smoking indoors.

The city banned smoking in most establishments in and around their premises decades ago, but not Uncle Joe's. It's a freestanding biker bar that was grandfathered in, exempting them from the new law. There's nothing the city can do about it. I've never bought the story, but the place has been here since the sixties doing whatever the hell it wants. Tonight it's where I'll be shooting a few shots of something stiff. Noelle is supposed to meet me here to commiserate with me after I got stood up again.

It's the second time in two weeks Seth has canceled on me, and it's a hit to the self-esteem. I should've expected it after the first time, but he assured me it wouldn't happen again. He insisted I get all dressed up and he'd take me to a nice restaurant downtown to make it up to me. We've been casually dating for two months after we connected on Tipsy's, a dating website. I joined on a whim after Tim, my boyfriend of three years, broke it off with me because he wanted to explore other women. I was devastated at the time.

Tim swore there was no other woman he was seeing while dating me, that the breakup was about him and not me. Oddly, I believed him. But it didn't hurt any less. How do you spend years with someone and then decide they're not enough of what you want when you don't even know what you want?

I was blindsided by his actions. I thought things were going in a good direction between us. We got along well. We hardly ever disagreed with each other. Sure the sex was mediocre, but none of my friends were having mind-blowing orgasms, so I assumed our sex life was normal. But I guess he was looking for a quality I didn't possess because he ended things just over six months ago.

Tim let me have the one-bedroom apartment we shared since I could afford it, and he moved out to rent a loft for himself. It helped me out more than it did him. I hate moving, plus I like the part of the art district I live in and don't want to leave. It's within walking distance to work, and it's surrounded by a variety of food places to eat. Tim didn't particularly like it here and told me so often. He preferred suburbia. I told him I was too young for that. He didn't like my job either, but that's a different story. Distraught, I went on the rebound.

And here I am at Uncle Joe's, ready to drink

away my sorrows. I've been a bit jaded when it comes to men. I'm ready to throw in the towel and be done with the entire species.

Noelle heard the despair in my voice when I called to tell her Seth stood me up for the last time. I'm not going to beg a man to stay with me, especially when the relationship is still so new. I just agreed to his excuse, like I always did, and wished him luck. Getting stood up so close to an emotional breakup is hard on the heart. My confidence is a bit fractured after what Tim did to me.

I eye the entrance to the bar as I tug down the hem of my minidress. Most people inside will be wearing denim and boots. I doubt anyone but me will be wearing a silk hunter green dress with matching high heels that scream "fuck me." I got dolled up for Seth tonight. I added wide waves to my long hair and even did my makeup better than I normally would. The humidity makes my hair look wild and sultry. I felt beautiful and wanted him to be pleased to see me. I wanted to be the only thing in the room he saw. I gained some weight after the breakup with Tim, and now every piece of clothing I have is bursting at the seams. This once slinky dress gives me newfound curves. I can't say I don't like them because I do. I feel sexy. More womanly.

I enter the dimly lit, smoky open room and make a beeline for the bar, hoping to sit between a rough around the edges guy who will appreciate my presence. My gaze scans the heads, looking for an open space to squeeze into, but my optimism fades quickly. The only available seat is next to a man who is already watching me. Our eyes connect and my heart flutters rapidly. He's dressed in business attire and appears clean-cut, like he runs a tight ship. He's a little out of place here, like me, and the exact opposite of what I want to be around tonight. Tim and Seth both wear dressy business attire. I don't want to sit next to someone who reminds me of them, but it seems to be the way the world works for me lately.

Nervously, I toy with my small purse in front of me. He's eating up the length of my body like he wants to feast on it. Awareness flutters down my spine. Maybe he'll buy me a drink. A surge of attraction passes between us and my stomach flips. Our eyes connect again when he's done observing me once more. My cheeks burn under his penetrating gaze as I walk toward him. Thank goodness the room has blue LED lights otherwise the deep red would be noticeable on my cheeks.

I drop my arms to hang at my sides. Swallowing back the knot in my throat, I continue forward and close the distance. He pulls the barstool out for me to sit. I offer him a timid smile and slide in. The bald bartender immediately places a white cocktail napkin in front of me and takes my order. The sleeves are torn off his denim shirt, and the tattoo on his bicep is in the old green ink that's hard to make out after forty years.

"Shot of tequila," I tell him, and he nods. "Make it a double, please."

"I'll have what she's having," the guy next to me says.

I hand the bartender my credit card and tell him to start a tab. He turns away, and the guy to my left turns to look at me. His gaze sears the side of my face. I pretend like I don't notice him, but that doesn't stop him. He leans in, and I hold my breath.

"Stood up?"

My eyes close shut. The universe is testing me.

I don't respond and remain facing forward. The last thing I'm going to do is tell a stranger my woes. It's embarrassing as it is, and I don't want to talk about it. But he doesn't take my silence as a hint.

"If the outfit didn't give it away, your drink order did."

I bob my head in defeat. "Is it obvious?" I ask and turn toward him. One corner of his mouth tugs up as he nods. "What kind of drink should I have gotten if I wasn't stood up?"

"A cosmo or a glass of wine. Not two shots of straight liquor." He pauses. "Sounds rough."

I notice the pack of menthol cigarettes to the left of him. Maybe sitting next to him wasn't such a bad outcome after all. I was hoping to bum one off someone since I don't usually carry them. The bartender places the clear liquid in front of me and a small cup of lime wedges, then he does the same for the man to my left before moving on to help another customer. The man sees me eyeing the carton and picks it up. He flips the top back and offers me one. I take it and thank him with a smile. He hands me the lighter and I place both on my napkin. I want my drink first.

"Life has been rough lately," I say. It's my trade for the smoke.

"For what it's worth, I'm glad he stood you up. It means I get to look at you. At least I'll appreciate it."

A knot forms in my throat. This guy is good.

Picking up the shot glass, I wonder for a moment if I manifested this encounter. As much as I want to be a bitch and curse the male population, the man doesn't deserve my wrath. It might have to do with the fact that he's a sight for sore eyes.

"Thank you."

He picks up his glass and says, "I can't let you drink alone."

"You're not. My best friend is on her way over," I tell him.

"Well, until then, you have me."

A bashful smile pulls at the corners of my mouth. His dark eyes twinkle with mischief, and the look calls out to me. He raises his glass. I lift mine and we tap them together without saying anything. We shoot them at the same time, then we each reach for a lime wedge, all while not wavering from each other's gaze.

"Is the guy who stood you up a boyfriend?" he asks.

He acts like he tossed back water; meanwhile, my throat is on fire and goose bumps are racing down my arms.

"I don't even know your name and you're asking me that? Are you always this nosy?"

He sucks the juice from the lime then tosses the peel on his napkin. "No. I usually like to watch others interact. But you walked in with a vengeance, and I had to get to know you."

"Lucky me," I say sarcastically.

He leans his elbow on the bar and meets my gaze. "My name is Leo," he says.

I swallow thickly. "Trista."

"So, is he, Trista?"

I study Leo, liking the way he's provoking me with his tone while pretending his questions are innocent.

"We'd only started seeing each other about two months ago. I'm going to call it off completely with him. I don't like being stood up. I wouldn't call him a boyfriend."

Leo squints. "A relationship that short wouldn't call for drinking shots with your best friend."

I sit up a little taller. I don't like feeling completely seen, and he makes me feel that way. I take in his navy-blue dress pants and think about how they shape his thighs.

"Were you stood up too?" I ask, taking the focus off me.

Leo smirks like he knows I'm trying to change the topic. "I'm here on business. My partner was too but had to head home. He's on the way to the airport now to catch a red-eye. I needed a drink and some food, and this place came up when I did a search on my phone."

"You're not from here?"

Leo shakes his head. "I live in Hawaii. I leave tomorrow afternoon. Do you live here?"

My brows rise as I nod. Now I'm intrigued. "What do you do?" I ask.

"I'm a restauranteur. People hire me to open their business. My client wants to bring a taste of the island to the downtown area. He's opening a restaurant in time for New Year's Eve. I'm here doing business on his behalf."

I reach for the cigarette and place the filter in my mouth. Leo already has the lighter in his hand and the flame lit for me.

"New Year's is this month." I pull in a drag and hold it for a moment before exhaling. "Where are you staying?"

"The Four Seasons," he says.

"Ritzy."

Leo shrugs. "I'm not complaining. My client pays for it. There's nothing wrong with living luxuriously."

The bartender comes back around and points a finger between the two of us. "Would you like anything else?"

Leo orders two more shots. This time they're on him.

"Where in the downtown area is the restaurant? What street?" I ask curiously.

"Lake Shore Drive," he says, and I perk up. "You know it?" he asks when he sees my reaction.

"Very well. I work the next street over. I'm redesigning a city block of store windows for the holiday season. So you'll be coming back to Chicago since the opening is only a couple of weeks away?"

Leo nods. "Maybe we'll run into each other again."

My gaze meets his unblinking one. It tickles the warmth in my lower belly. "Serendipity." I smile. "There's a lot of people in the city. Do you believe in happenstance?" I say, flirting a little.

"I believe anything is possible," Leo says.

"Let's cheers to that," I say and lift the shot glass. I hold one lime in my other hand.

We look at each other, and my heart begins to flutter again. We tap the glasses together and shoot our drinks back. My eyes water, and I blink rapidly from the harsh liquor. I bite into the lime and welcome the sourness as I swallow it back.

Placing the empty glass on the bar counter, I say, "The guy I was dating for three years decided he wanted to explore the ocean." I pause to lick my lips and decide to go the whole nine yards. "Then I got stood up by this new guy. That's the real reason I'm here."

"Ouch. It's a good thing I ordered another round," Leo says. "It's been one hit after another for you."

CHAPTER TWO
TRISTA

He isn't wrong.

I dump the lime into the shot glass and push it away. I'm surprised I'm divulging so much information that I pick up my phone to check where Noelle is. I send her a quick text.

"What a total cliché I am tonight," I say. Though, I'm not sad about it. I'm in rebound mode. "I got dumped and need to get drunk."

"It's a classic story," he says, shaking his head but going along with me.

My smile widens. I like how he responds, like it's a rite of passage. My phone chimes, and I reach for it. Swiping it open, I read Noelle's text and deflate. Her car won't start, and she needs to have it towed before the yard closes for the weekend. I offer help, but she says to have a drink on her and text her when I get home. I put my cell phone away just as the bartender brings the next round of shots.

Leo cautiously slides a shot glass toward me.

"Judging by your face, I'd say there's more shit news."

"My best friend can't make it now."

I pick up the shot for what it is and study it. A series of shitty, unfortunate events. I fall into a fit of giggles wondering how this is my luck right now. The nicotine combined with the liquor makes me feel a little tipsy already. I look at Leo. He makes me blush.

"I'm glad you ordered this. It's like you knew." I tease, hoping he'll get my drift.

Leo's knee bounces between us. He blinks and our glasses tap once again. He doesn't tear his eyes from mine. It feels intimate, like he's stripping me down. I bite into a lime wedge then place it on the white napkin. A flush spreads through me. I exhale and turn toward Leo.

"Now that you know about my love life, what about you?" I ask. "Are you married?"

I instantly regret my question. I wanted the focus off me, but then I stupidly ask him his relationship status. It's like a gateway question for more.

Yet, as I look at him, I can't deny that I'm not interested in him, or actually feel wrong for asking. Leo is so damn good-looking. He has this calm, seductive pull to him that I feel in the center of my chest. I'm attracted to him. Though, I'm not sure I have it in me to make a move after all the rejection I've endured recently.

"No, I'm not. I'm not dating or seeing anyone."

"You're probably lying," I say, and his shoulders

bounce as he laughs at my response. I look for his left hand. "What? You probably are."

"Trista, the man-hater." He pokes fun at me.

I smirk and unapologetically admit the truth. "I am a man-hater tonight. But do you blame me?"

His gaze roams over my face. "No, I don't. But not all men are like that. The ex leaving is a blessing in disguise. You want to be with someone who knows there isn't more than you. He won't find what he's looking for. His type is never satisfied."

I need to slow down. The fire from the shots is warming my veins and making me feel even more tipsy. I take one more puff of my cigarette then offer the rest to Leo. He leans in, and I inhale his cologne as the spicy scent curls around me. Leo brings the cigarette to his mouth and places his lips right where I had mine. He eyes me over the embers at the tip. Music plays over the speakers in the background, and I notice a band setting up. I realize Friday night has live music. Anticipation makes me smile. I love watching live music.

"How were you getting home tonight? Your friend?" Leo asks.

I shake my head and look back at him. "Uber. At least I know they won't let me down."

A smirk curves one corner of his mouth. Dry humor is what occurs when I'm going through things. Not everyone gets it, but Leo doesn't seem bothered by it.

Leo lifts two fingers toward the bartender and orders another round. I was going to slow down, but fuck it. I like the state I'm floating into. I'm not driving, and anyway, Leo is good company right now.

"Know what you're in need of?" Leo asks, dabbing out the cigarette.

"I can't wait to hear this."

He leans in close and whispers near my ear, "A good, hard fuck. A no commitment, no strings attached one-night stand."

My eyes widen and my lips part as a chuckle leaves my mouth. Leo is the most forward man I've ever met in my life. I pull back, a shyness creeping over me. My cheeks are blooming with heat. He doesn't blink as he watches me, and it makes my chest burn with tension.

"Obviously. But I'm not a one-night stand kind of person."

"Bullshit." He tips his head toward me curiously. "Everyone is. Why are you the one exception?" His gaze roams over me and eats me up.

"Strangers don't have the chemistry lovers do. The sex is barely performed at fifty percent. It's not bad, but it's not mind-blowing enough to make me do it often. When there's a serious relationship, it just feels different. Then I want it often."

The tequila is making me ramble, yet I don't stop.

"Is he just not attracted to me anymore? Is that what it is?"

"It's definitely not you," Leo says quickly. He leans in close, and the back of my neck tingles at his proximity. "I can't take my eyes off you, Trista. I was drawn to you the moment you stepped inside."

Leave it to a stranger to make my emotions rise to the surface. I reach for the fourth shot and pass the other to Leo. After this one, I'm going to take a break. I'm past tipsy and feeling extra good. I want to make sure some of my common sense remains intact.

"The relationship doesn't have to be serious for the sex to feel good," he says, his voice low. It sends tingles down my spine. "Maybe you're just finding duds. Not everyone knows how to handle a woman's body."

His implication is loud and clear. The temptation tastes delicious. Leo wants me to know he knows how to please a woman. It's been a while since I've truly flirted with anyone that I forgot what it feels like.

I raise the shot and say, "Here's to finding a stud."

Slamming the empty glass on the counter, I shake my head, letting him know I need a break.

A cool gust of wind breezes past my back. I shoot a glance over my shoulder and do a double take at who's walking through the front door. My jaw drops. I didn't anticipate seeing anyone I know here tonight. I frown, wondering if I'm drunk when I realize that I'm not. Clenching my eyes shut, I swivel around and pray he didn't notice me. I sense Leo watching me for a long second before he turns to look at the entrance.

Why the hell is Tim here? I didn't think this was his type of scene. The last time I saw him was the day he moved out.

"Your love life is riveting. Who's this one?"

Exhaling a tight breath, I say dryly, "The ocean explorer."

Leo barks out a laugh. I lift my eyes to his and give him a half smile.

"He's coming this way," Leo says without moving his mouth.

"Of course he is," I mutter under my breath.

"Actually, there's no other empty barstools. The place is filling up. They're going to sit on the other end of the bar."

My stomach tightens. "They?"

"Looks like he's got a date," Leo says, and I try not to react too much to the news. He looks down at me and pauses. "You were meant to sit next to me tonight. I'm going to be your wingman."

My brows bunch together when I hear my name being called.

"Trista?"

Fuck.

This means Tim did see me. Now I have no choice but to address him. I must be the quintessential ex-girlfriend who can't catch a break after being dumped repeatedly.

Sucking in a deep breath, I plaster on fake joy. "Tim," I say, acting surprised. "Hi. Ah, how are you?"

I realize my heart is racing and I'm starting to

panic. Tim eyes the length of me. I shoot a fleeting look at the woman next to him. She's naturally gorgeous, and pint-size. It boggles my mind how Tim has a date and I can't seem to land one. I'm seriously beginning to question my capabilities.

"I thought that was you when I walked in. You look nice. Real good."

I flatten my lips into a thin smile. "Thanks."

Am I supposed to say you too? Because I don't want to compliment him. After all, this is the guy who left me to go find better.

I'm still salty.

"You're so dressed up," he begins, and my stomach drops.

Leo whispers in my ear for me to play along before he reaches around behind me.

"I'm Leo, Trista's boyfriend," he says, and I can't stop the shocked expression from filling my face. Leo puts his hand out to shake Tim's. Heat blossoms the bridge of my nose. Even my neck is burning. Tim looks at me oddly then places his hand in Leo's.

This is what Leo meant when he said he'd be my wingman.

He's going to play my boyfriend.

I look at Leo's side profile. At least it won't be hard pretending I find him attractive, because I already do.

"Nice to meet you," Tim says hesitantly.

Leo sits back down and places his palm on my hip affectionally. "We had dinner reservations, but the restaurant overbooked. We decided to skip eating and came here for drinks instead."

Tim nods then moves his date to the open seats.

I turn toward Leo and mouth, "Thank you." He nods in understanding. I'm thankful Tim doesn't know the truth. It would make me feel even lower.

Without thinking, I lean forward to give Leo a kiss as a thank-you. His lips are cool and taste tart, and it's what makes me realize what I'm doing all too late. I try to pull back, but he doesn't let me. Leo palms the back of my head and smushes our lips together. He allows just enough space to slip his tongue into my mouth to tangle with mine. Lust pools in my pussy, and my body illuminates with desire. Just as fast as it starts, it's over.

Leo slides another shot over, and I take it without hesitation. He chuckles quietly. It burns going down and I welcome it.

"Want to share a cigarette?" he asks.

I nod immediately. After my ex walked into Uncle Joe's, and me kissing Leo, tequila doesn't seem strong enough for the job.

"If you're not into one-night stands, I bet you don't kiss on the first date either," Leo says.

CHAPTER THREE
TRISTA

L eo's question causes me to question myself.

I was with Tim for three years. Before that, I was in college and that didn't count. Everyone fucked everyone then.

I'm not sure what I don't do on dates. Was I into one-night stands and kissing? Or was I not? Leaning closer, I turn my entire body to face him.

"I'm not sure what I do on dates. Tim was my first real boyfriend, and we happened out of college by accident."

A cigarette dangles between his lips. Leo cups the end to light it and then pulls in a drag. Veins protrude down the column of his neck. It makes me wonder how old he is.

Exhaling, Leo says, "You don't know what you like yet."

The knot in my throat grows thicker. He's reading me like a book, and I don't know if I like it.

I swallow and subtly shake my head. This stranger has me all flustered and giddy.

"He keeps looking at you," he says, and takes a puff of the cigarette before handing it off to me.

I shrug, dejection coasting through me. The tequila is hitting me in my emotions and making me say more than I probably should.

"He can look all he wants." I take a puff and hand the cigarette back. "It will never be the same with him even if my heart wasn't hurting."

"If he wanted you back, would you go?"

No. It's my first thought, and that surprises me. Regardless of how I've been mourning our relationship, the truth is, I couldn't be with Tim again. Running into him solidifies that. My heart doesn't feel the same toward him. I feel differently about him now. I'm hurt. He wanted to see if there was better out there when I should be the best thing in his life.

"No, I don't think I could." This night is starting to feel like a revelation. I meet Leo's eyes. "You're a good bestie fill-in, you know. Like I went to bestie therapy. I feel a little relieved."

Leo takes a pull on the cigarette and hands it to me. "Stay with me tonight. Come back to my hotel room with me, and in return I'll play the attentive boyfriend in front of Tim. I'll make him regret his decision."

I stare in utter shock. Leo doesn't blink.

This sort of thing only ever happens in the movies.

My heart is pumping faster, and the urge to take him up on his offer is strong. This is what I need, right? A hot and dirty one-night stand. And to show Tim that I'm more than enough.

I'll have to send Noelle my location if I go.

"What do you say?" he asks.

I bite my lip. A part of me wants to make Tim jealous. I want to show him what he's missing out on. I'm a scorned woman, after all.

"Why?" I ask. "Why do this?"

"Why not?" he replies. "It'll make for an eventful night, and we both get something out of it. Neither one of us have plans. I'm leaving to go back to Hawaii tomorrow. It's the perfect no strings attached one-night stand."

My chest flutters with temptation. I wonder if Leo ever considered law school with how persistent he is.

He leans in and lowers his voice as he says, "Let me be your first one-night stand so you have something to compare the others to."

Heat rises to my cheeks. I try not to turn away. "You're going to set the bar?"

Leo scoots closer to me, and I feel the heat of his body next to mine. I like the way temptation feels. It makes my chest burn with desire.

"Stay with me and find out."

"I don't even know how old you are."

"Age is just a number. We're both of age and consenting, and that's all that matters." He glances above my head quickly then back down to me.

"Tim's date just walked away. I presume to go to the restroom. I'm going to the men's room. If Tim comes over here and talks to you while I'm gone, then you're coming with me." He looks over my head. "I'll play the fake boyfriend either way. Make your decision quickly."

It's instant. "I'll do it."

"Time starts now."

His eyes bear into mine with promises he intends to keep. Leo bends down and kisses the top of my forehead and then walks away.

Playing into this charade, I face forward and act like my ex isn't in the bar. I doubt Tim will talk to me. I flag the bartender down and order a mixed drink.

"It's good to see you, Trista," Tim says.

I turn to my side as Tim slides into the empty barstool next to me. He looks over me, his tongue practically wagging. He made it a whole ten seconds before engaging, which surprises me since he's here with a date. I really didn't think we'd talk alone.

The bartender places my drink in front of me, and I take a sip.

I give Tim a friendly smile before replying, "You too."

"I can't take my eyes off you," he admits. "You look different. Whatever you did, it's working for you."

I flatten my lips. It's called emotional stress eating. However, I'm not going to tell him that. Then

I'd have to admit how much weight I've gained, and that's not happening.

"I didn't know you have a wandering eye. What does your girlfriend think about that?"

"She's not my girlfriend. She's just a friend I'm getting drinks with. I've never slept with her." I take another sip of my drink, surprisingly unbothered. "You know, I was thinking about calling you. I miss having you around. I was thinking maybe we could get coffee or dinner sometime."

Then why haven't you? I want to ask, but I don't. Tim's heated gaze drops to my mouth and it does nothing for me the way Leo's does.

Interesting.

"I'm seeing Leo," I say, going along with the story. "I don't think I should be getting coffee with you."

"He doesn't have to know."

My eyes pop wide and my jaw drops. Despite the relationship being fake, anger ignites inside of me. His sense of entitlement makes me fume. Was he like this with other women while we were dating? I'm not sure I want to know.

"Leo is my boyfriend," I reiterate.

"I didn't think you'd move on so quickly," he says, and I can't believe he just said that. He has some nerve.

"Did you think I would sneak behind his back for you?" I ask.

Tim gawks at me. "Yeah, I did. It's me," he says arrogantly, like it's obvious. "Our breakup is still in the early stages. The rules are different. We have a lot of history. I was thinking we can talk things out."

A week ago, heck, yesterday, I would have said yes, but this mysterious man named Leo appeared in my world and changed things up. Now the answer is no.

"I can't," I tell him. "It feels sneaky. Like I'm being deceitful."

"Where did you meet him so quickly?" Tim asks, and I'm thankful Leo told me why he's in Chicago.

"Not that it's any of your business, but he's opening a restaurant for a client downtown. He was picking up lunch at the same place I was, and we hit it off."

Tim studies me, and I pray he can't tell that I'm lying.

"Will you at least call me? Can we start there?" he pleads.

I'm about to take it to the next level when Leo appears. He wraps a possessive arm around my waist and buries his nose in my neck.

"Looks like you're all mine," he whispers for only me to hear. My nipples harden beneath the dress. Thank goodness he can't see them. Tim looks uncomfortable as he watches.

"Keeping Trista company, Tim?" Leo asks him. He doesn't take his hand off me as he sits down and pulls me into his lap. I sort of like it.

"We're catching up. We have a lot of history between us."

There's a pause, and it's awkward.

"You know, I need to use the rest room now that you're back," I say, using it as the perfect opportunity to take a break from the weird tension. "All those tequila shots are hitting me. Want to order one more and then we'll go?"

Leo nods. Tim's date returns and joins us. She points in the direction of the ladies' room. I nearly sprint there and relieve myself immediately in the small bathroom. I need to come up with an exit strategy. Not that I'm trying to escape to Leo's hotel just yet, but I need to get away from Tim. Maybe Leo will want to go to another bar. Or get something to eat. I'm pretty drunk and could use some carbs.

As I'm drying my hands, the door swings open and in walks Leo. He's tall and his shoulders are broad. He fills out his dress shirt so there's not any breathing room left.

"What are you doing in here?" I whisper.

My teeth dig into my bottom lip, and I wait in anticipation to see what his next move is.

CHAPTER FOUR
LEO

When Trista first walked into the bar, I was drawn to her like a bear to honey.

She is the most beautiful woman I've ever seen. I was captivated. She took my breath away.

Imagine my luck when she sat right next to me. I started sweating. My heartbeat was pumping against my ribs. My cock came to life, and I got this strange, brewing tension in my stomach.

I came to this hole-in-the-wall bar on a whim after my partner had a family emergency and had to fly out. While Uncle Joe's isn't the type of place I normally get drunk in, I didn't come here to make friends. All I wanted was a drink and maybe something to eat. The last thing I expected was to find a woman for the night who looks like Trista.

Her green eyes remind me of someone who's sad in the summertime. They're missing that sparkle. She makes me want to put the life back into them. And her body, fuck, she walks with a body that should be praised. Her blond hair is frizzy and wild, and her pouty mouth is downright adorable.

Then her ex appeared, throwing a curveball into the mix. He ate her alive with his eyes, and I couldn't stand to see it. He doesn't deserve her after what Trista told me. So after a few shots of liquid courage, I ask her to stay the night. She wants a hot and dirty one-night stand. I have what she's looking for. I convince Trista to let me act as her boyfriend. Though, it didn't seem like she needed much convincing. I'll show her ex what he lost. Coming from a man, I know he's regretting his decision by the way he's looking at her.

I step into the bathroom as Trista is washing her hands. She's startled to see me. I shut and lock the door then spin around and stride over to where she's standing. I didn't appreciate the way little Timmy spoke to me at the bar, insinuating shit, so I'm going to eat Trista out until she can barely walk. When he sees how flushed she is, he'll think I fucked her in the bathroom.

Trista steps backward until I'm pushing her against the wall with my body. My hips press into her soft belly. I cup the side of her neck and tip her head back, rotating my hips into hers so she feels how hard I am for her.

"He wanted me to have coffee with him and not tell you."

"He wanted you to cheat," I state. It's obvious to a man what he's after. "Sounds like he's regretting his decision."

The corners of her pouty mouth lift just a fraction. "Where does he think you are right now?"

"He doesn't know I left. His date was talking to him when I walked away."

I feel her swallow under my palm. My gaze falls to her mouth and I decide that's enough talking. I slant my lips over hers, and she opens immediately, allowing me to slip my tongue inside and tangle around hers. Desire zips up my spine. She strokes me back with the same intensity and it turns me on higher. Trista drapes her arms over my shoulders and deepens the kiss. Passion brews between us. I can't wait to get her back to my room so I can take my time with her.

My hands skim down her sides and over her round ass. I groan at her softness. She has two balloons back here I hadn't seen until she walked away. My tongue was nearly wagging by the time she rounded the corner and disappeared. I watched them bounce with each step she took, fantasizing what my tongue would feel like between them.

I press my fingers into her softness and moan into her mouth. She's like holding a pillow I can't wait to bury my head in. Trista rubs her pussy on me. I bet she would come so quick at the touch of my fingers since she hasn't had sex in months based on what she told me. She reaches between our bodies and strokes my cock over my dress pants. My hips press into her palm and my dick swells blissfully.

Trista lets out a kitten purr and wraps her fingers

around my tip. She squeezes and I hiss in a breath. A shot of lust shoots straight to my balls. Breaking away from the kiss, she stares at me with glossy eyes. Trista licks her lips. I can't wait to feel those lips wrapped around my dick. She tastes like I'm about to become addicted, and that worries me.

"Pull your dress up," I say, breathing heavily. "And spread your legs."

Normally, I'd let the woman suck me off before I fuck her, but since Trista is coming home with me, we have all night for that. Right now, I just want a taste of her, and I'm not leaving without it. By the time I'm done with her, she's going to ask if she can suck my cock as a thank-you.

Trista bunches the tight dress in her fists and shimmies it up to settle on her waist. My mouth waters at the sexy sight before me, and I swallow thickly with need. She's all flesh and thickness. I want to get lost in her curves. She's wearing black lace underwear and matching thigh-high stockings.

"Leave the stockings on. Take the panties off and step out of them."

My voice is low and guttural, but she doesn't question me. As soon as the material hits the floor, I fall to my knees. Her eyes widen down at me. Trista reaches out, but I grab both of her wrists and pin them to the sides of her body. I stare up at her.

"What are you doing?" she whispers.

"Making sure you know you're coming home with me."

I lean forward and kiss her pussy, delving my

tongue between her lips. Her back arches, and she lets out a deep, long moan. She squirms against my face with nowhere to go but to feel my tongue on her clit. Her strain against me dissipates and her stance miraculously widens. I do it again, this time stroking further between her pussy lips that she's angling her hips in my direction now. I smile inwardly, proud one stroke was all it took. Letting go of her wrists, I rub myself all over her opening, and she bucks against my face. She's slippery and juicy. I pull her swollen lips back with the pads of my thumbs and lick her clean. The bathroom echoes with the slurping sound my mouth makes as I eat her out. I go to town and her thighs tremble. She's dripping down my chin and rubbing her pussy over my stubble. She's already close to orgasming. Trista cups the sides of my head and holds me to her. I love when a woman takes control like this. Like she knows exactly what she wants and will use me to get it. My cock is like a stone hanging painfully between my legs.

"Leo." She pants.

My name is a whisper on her lips.

I hum my response with my mouth suctioned around her clit. Trista sucks in a breath. Using her wetness, I coat my index finger and then slowly insert it into her entrance. Her pussy walls are warm and pillowy soft, like a teenage dream. I can't wait to be inside of her. Before she gets too much pleasure, I pull my lips off her clit and glance up. Her jaw hangs in astonishment.

"What? What are you doing?" she asks, panting.

"Missing my mouth?" I ask as I finger her.

Her jaw falls open wider. She nods rapidly. Her pussy is so close to my face that I can smell her pleasure. Pulling my finger out, I push back in and curl it to press on her wall.

"When I'm done eating you, we're getting the bill and leaving."

"Yes," she says, nodding. And that's enough for me.

I dive between her legs again and suction hard around her clit. I French-kiss her pussy and draw every ounce of pleasure from her body until she's falling over the edge. Her legs shake. Trista gyrates on my mouth as I finger-fuck her pussy and work to suck the orgasm from her clit. She lets out a guttural moan and explodes on my tongue. She runs her fingers through my hair and pulls on the strands. I look up to watch her and see the hard outline of her nipples. Her breathing levels, and she lets go of my hair.

Sitting back on my knees, I break away from her pussy and find myself breathing hard. She's dripping down her inner thigh. Without thinking, I wipe it up with my fingers then lick them clean. She watches me.

"Wow," is all she says. "Fuck."

Trista tries to tug her dress down, but she doesn't have the strength. I help her until she's covered enough to walk out.

"Can you hand me those?" she asks breathlessly.

Reaching between us, I pick up her panties and feel a damp spot on them. I bunch them into a ball and stuff them into my pocket, grinning to myself. That's proof she was turned on by me.

"You better not sell those for cash," she tells me.

Standing up, I lean in close to see if she'll kiss me after I ate her out. When she doesn't move or flinch, I close the distance and give her a thorough, deep kiss.

She takes all of it.

"I'm going to fuck your panties when I go back home," I say against her mouth.

"Then you better give me something of yours before you leave so I can do the same."

A low growl escapes me. I wrap my arm around Trista's waist and tug her to me. We step in front of the mirror and Trista notices the flush of color in her cheeks and how swollen her lips are. Even her chest has a hint of red. I watch her throat bob, then she meets my gaze in the mirror. She turns and reaches up to try to fix my disheveled hair. One minute ago she was ripping it out of my head. I let her do her thing and look into her eyes. There's a stillness about her that I'm drawn to.

"I feel like I should say thank you," she says, her breath wispy.

"You will later when we're back in my room."

Trista drops her arms and I lead the way with her hand in mine. I unlock the door, then walk back toward the main room. We turn a corner that leads to where we were previously seated. Little Timmy notices us immediately and sits up straighter. He wears a curious frown. He eyes both of us suspiciously. I hope the woman he's with isn't his girlfriend. He's shown his attention to everything in the room but her. If Trista notices, she doesn't give it away that she does. She seems to be in her own world. My eyes meet Timmy's for the briefest moment, and I can taste the hatred he has for me simply because I have something he wants. I'm wearing her pussy all over my mouth, and I'm sure he can see it.

The number of people in the bar has grown, and it's getting stuffy. Perfect time to exit.

I raise my arm to get the bartender's attention. I request her tab be added to mine and then ask for the check.

My flight leaves in ten hours. I want to spend nine of them in Trista.

I steal a look at Trista. Her eyes glitter. She's sitting on the barstool and leaning back on the countertop, studying me.

"I feel like I just got my second wind," Trista says.

CHAPTER FIVE
LEO

"Good, because you're going to need it," I say, and she shakes her head. "What is it?"

"I never do anything like this," she says near my ear. "I feel like my body is humming. Unless it's the tequila."

The grin on my face grows. A shadow moves in the corner of my eye. I look over Trista's shoulder and see her ex walking toward us. My eyes lower to slits. Timmy watched me ask for the check a moment ago, so he must know we're leaving. I wonder if he's going to try and shoot his shot with her again.

"Incoming," I say under my breath.

Trista stands and nervously moves her hair behind her shoulder. Timmy stops on the other side of her as the bartender hands me the check. I place my credit card on the clipboard without reading the total and then lean closer to Trista. She's forced to turn her back to me. I try to listen to what they're saying, but the bar is loud, and I can bet Timmy is purposely being quiet and sneaky. Taking out my cell phone, I send a quick text to my driver that I'm ready for pickup. That way he'll be waiting for us outside when we leave.

"Darling," I say, signing my name on the receipt. I place the pen down. "Are you ready to leave?"

Trista looks at me and nods. "Yes."

It comes out lusty.

"My place or yours?" I ask.

Her eyes flicker. "Yours."

Even though we're in character, I can tell she likes that I called her Darling. Her lashes fall to her cheeks, and she glances away to pick up her purse. Timmy stares at me. His searing gaze burns a hole on the side of my cheek, but I pay him no attention. I have three sisters. They give death glares worse than anyone I know. If I didn't convince Trista to run in the other direction of Timmy after how she was treated, they would kill me in my sleep. So why not run her straight to my bed.

Timmy leans in to give Trista a hug, and I see red. It takes every ounce of strength I have not to rear back and punch him right in the face. I remind myself that this is a fake relationship, and I'm not going to start a bar fight in honor of that. But it pisses me off no less. He's asking for trouble with that kind of sense of entitlement. He needs to keep his hands off what's not his. The way I see it, he threw her away. One man's trash is another man's treasure.

I tug on her hip, and it doesn't take much to whisk Trista away.

"Thank you," she whispers once we step outside the double doors.

My driver is exactly where I knew he'd be. He spots me walking toward the black Land Rover and gets out to open the door. I have Trista step in front of me so she gets in first. Then I walk around to the other side and get in, thanking my driver. We pull away, and I put up the partition for privacy. My hotel is around the corner, so it won't take long to get there.

"I wanted to break his neck when he put his hands on you."

"I know. I could feel the tension radiating from your body."

I frown at her. "You could?" She nods. "I knew you wouldn't like it. You sort of remind me of the macho, possessive type. I tried to pull away, but he held me tighter. I was so glad you asked me if I was ready to leave."

She's not wrong about being that kind of man. "My woman is mine. I don't want anyone touching her. It's not out of insecurity either. It's out of respect." I pause. "He doesn't respect others."

Trista turns toward me. Her knees tap mine as we turn a corner. "You know, when he was talking to me before we left, I realized he never made me feel in three years what you did in two minutes in that bathroom. Not nearly as close."

My brows rise. "That means he never got to experience you the way I just did. Pity for him."

Trista slides closer to me. She leans up to capture my lips with hers, then cups my bulge and rubs her palm over my cock, massaging my heavy sack at the same time. I widen my thighs to give her more access.

"The better my partner feels, the better the sex will be," I tell her. "Make me feel good and watch how I fuck you into another state of mind."

Trista shivers, and I like the effect I have over her. Blindly, she guides my hand to her breast to touch her nipple. I can't wait to get my mouth on them. They've teased me all night. Trista has large breasts, and I love fat nipples. I'm hoping she has them. I want to suck on them while I fuck her. If I had to guess her cup size, I'd say she's one of those bigger letters, like E or H or something.

"I'm going to rip this dress off of you," I tell her. My balls are going to be blue by the time I get her undressed.

"I've never had my clothes torn from me before either," she says seductively.

I give her a look that promises I'll do just that and more.

Thank God we're here. The Land Rover comes to a stop in front of the Four Seasons. We're out of the car and in the penthouse suite in a matter of minutes.

Trista takes in the floor-to-ceiling windows that overlook the city. The room is bougie, but I love it.

There's a balcony with a jacuzzi, a spa bathroom, and a master bedroom with a king-size bed. She steps out of her heels as she walks. Before she can pull the zipper down on her dress, I walk up behind her and reach around to the front to tuck my fingers into the top of her dress. With my chest pressed to her back, I give one good tug and tear the dress from her body. She gasps. The material falls in a heap at her feet. My lips part at how beautiful she is. I cup her breasts and rub my throbbing cock against her ass, struggling with the need to be inside of her and the need to draw out the pleasure.

"I'll buy you a new one," I tell her as I pepper her neck with kisses. She smells so good I want to bite her.

"I don't care about the dress."

I nip at her neck with my teeth and stroke her with my tongue. I twist her nipples between my fingers, causing her head to loll back onto my chest. Trista reaches behind me and grabs whatever part of my body she can touch. My cock swells further. I can't wait to be inside of her. I can feel in the way she grips me how much she wants me, and it lures out a commanding side of me. When I told her that one-night stands can be exactly like this, I meant that it only works when two people have the same hunger.

Thankfully, we do.

"Do you have any condoms?" I ask. I don't want to wait another minute to be in her pussy.

"One," she says breathlessly.

"I have three. I get to fuck you four times before you leave." She purrs at my response, and a little giggle rolls off her lips. "What's so funny?"

"You're going to come four times in one night?" she asks in disbelief. "I don't think I've even orgasmed that many times in one night."

She can't see the grin that spreads across my face. I press it against the side of her neck and kiss her. Trista doesn't know who she's dealing with. I consider sex a sport. If I didn't have to be back in Hawaii, I'd keep her locked in the hotel all weekend with me and come so many times she'd lose count. I don't know much about her, but what I do know is that she's the kind of woman I can get lost in.

"Is that a challenge, darling?" I ask, wrapping my arms around her. "I've already made you come once."

She takes a deep breath and turns around to face me. Trista places her arms around my shoulders and leans into me. Her huge breasts press against my chest like balloons. She looks up with seduction in her eyes, and all I can think is that I'm fucked.

"Tonight is a night of firsts for me. Let's see what you got, hotshot."

The animal in me awakens. I'm going to ruin her for any other guy she fucks after me.

"Take my clothes off," I tell her. Her hands immediately fly to my belt. "Good girl. I want you to undress me and then get on your knees."

Trista licks her lips and moves quickly. I notice the goose bumps on her arms. I'm pleased she's not repulsed by the idea of blowing me. Not every woman actually likes to do it.

Once I step out of my pants, she moves to the buttons on my shirt and has me naked in the blink of an eye. I reach for her, but she takes my wrist and has me follow her like a lost puppy. I'm about to question myself when we stop in front of the open window. She drops to her knees and places her hands on my thighs. I look out at the city. I got lost in the twinkling skyline last night.

I look down at this beautiful girl and cup her jaw. She opens her mouth and takes all of me in one gulp. Her tongue wraps around my shaft and coats my cock like it's a heated blanket. It sends chills down my spine. My dick swells with desire. Trista suctions her lips and gives me a wicked blow job that makes me grind my molars together. She sucks my dick like it makes her happy to. If she puts this much effort into a blow job, I can't wait to see how it'll feel when I'm between her legs.

I reach for one of the foil packets and tear it open with my teeth. My balls are tight and aching. We can take the other fuck sessions slower, but right now, I need to be in her.

Trista pulls back, and I roll the condom on. My dick is so hard. She looks up at me with doe eyes and walks back on her hands and feet. I eye her like prey, tracking her with each step I take. She stops on the sheepskin rug and lies on her back. Trista lets out a sigh and drops her knees open, exposing herself to me.

Falling to my knees, I crawl up her body. I give one good lick to her pussy because I can't pass it without doing so, then I rise back up on my knees. My palm runs down the inside of her thigh, enamored with her. I can't remember a time when I've been so ravenous for a woman.

I palm my cock and run the tip around her pussy to lube it up. "I want to hear you," I tell her. Trista nods. The sounds she makes dictate what I do. I need to know what she likes and doesn't like.

Pressing the tip to her entrance, I push inside until the crown is in. Her tender pink lips are swollen and puffy. I pull them back with my thumbs and watch her pussy swallow my cock. I can't tear my eyes away as she takes all of me. I let out a long moan and dig my fingers into her thighs. Damn, she feels good. I pull back then surge back in a couple of times to get her adjusted. Trista throws her arms above her head. She lets out a sexy sigh, and I love the sound of it. Her nipples harden while I stroke her clit. I pump my hips into hers with small quick thrusts. Trista begins panting. I want to bring her to the brink so I can tear into her like an animal and fuck her hard. The heels of her feet dig into my backside.

"Kiss me," she whispers.

CHAPTER SIX
LEO

I drop on top of her to find her lips.

I devour her kiss and drive my hips into hers with a desperate need that I can't stop. Trista hikes a leg over my hip and meets me thrust for thrust. She rubs her clit over my mound, and I grind into her when she does. She gasps when I hit that one spot and melts under me. The pleasure overtaking my body is intense. It's electric and addicting, and for a fleeting second, that worries me.

Trista struggles in my grip. I'm holding her wrists to the floor above her head. She's locked under me and can't escape. She wiggles, but I continue to surge into her warm pussy.

"Leo," she says against my lips. "I want you to fuck me harder."

My eyes open and I find she's already looking at me. Deep down I like when a woman likes sex a little rougher. It's a turn-on. Though, not many do.

Vanilla missionary is their favorite flavor. I don't hate it, but it's not my favorite.

I take Trista's lips and pound into her, slapping my thighs against her backside. Her back bows, but I don't relent. The sounds we're making are unmistakable. If anyone heard us, they'd know two people were having sex like rabbits.

Desire is floating through me, and the spark of an orgasm blooms in my balls. I groan and proceed to fuck Trista a little harder.

"Oh fuck, Trist," I gush.

I can't finish saying her name. Pleasure slams into me like its karma for what I'm doing to her.

"You're going to make me come," she whispers. "Oh, oh, oh. Oh yeah."

She causes another set of chills to roll down my spine. I work her pussy, rolling my cock into her with finesse. She's so slick and wet that I'm drowning in her. Her lips part and she makes little sounds of pleasure as she pulsates around my dick.

"Is that it?" I ask, my voice low and guttural. My cock throbs as I taunt her. "Is that it right there?"

Trista rubs her body against mine, squirming in desire. She nods her head. "Make me come, Leo." She pants, and says again, "Make me come."

I slam into her clit and her body clenches. Her eyes gloss over after I do it again. The moment I feel her pussy repeatedly tighten around mine, her eyes roll closed and I know she's coming. Trista yells out, crying in pleasure. Her kisses have me famished. I pump into her and come immediately. I can't stop my hips from jacking into hers. Trista works her sweet pussy on me, and I come so hard I don't recognize the sounds leaving me. This orgasm easily slides into one of the best ones I've ever had.

"Fuck," I groan. "Fuck, Trista."

I release my hold on her wrists and prop myself up on my elbows. She wraps her arms around my shoulders and runs her hands over my back.

"I wanted to touch you so bad," she says. "I wanted to feel you fuck me."

A growl vibrates in my chest. "Why didn't you just tell me? I would have let go."

She swallows and shakes her head. A blush paints her cheeks. "I liked what you were doing to me and didn't want to stop it."

I bend down and kiss her lips. "Next time."

I sit back and pull the condom off, then get up to throw it away. But I'm not done with her yet. I grab a few more condoms, then I walk back into the living room and wave her over to me. There's a mock fireplace on one side of the room and a view of the skyline on the other. I take Trista's hand and pull her into my lap on the chaise lounge.

Our legs sandwich each other's. I cup her ass cheeks and press her against my semihard cock. What I wouldn't give to feel the real thing. Trista gasps as my thigh pushes into her clit. She's dripping wet. I want to make her come again, and now is the best time to do it while she's still drowsy with pleasure.

"I want to feel you come on me like this," I tell

her, and surge my thigh against her pussy. "Use me to make yourself feel good. Seeing you orgasm like this is going to make me fuck you again."

She pulls back. "You mean use you like a pillow?"

I nod, feeling hot desire curl in my chest. Watching a woman orgasm is a guilty pleasure of mine.

"The more you use me, the harder my dick will get."

"Tell me what you like," she says. Trista doesn't hold back and situates herself. Her knee pushes into my balls, and it feels good when she rocks into me.

"The way your sexy body moves over me. How I can feel every part of your pussy open and wet. You dripping down my thigh. How you squeeze your legs to make it feel good."

She reaches for my dick. Her fingers wrap around my width and her thumb slides across the precum pearled on the tip.

She kisses my neck. "You do like this, don't you?"

"Fuck yes."

Trista grips my dick a little tighter. I clench my teeth, trying to hold back the pleasure it creates. I take one of her nipples into my mouth and lick around the pink part. She moans, and her pussy is soaked. She's slipping all over my thigh as she uses me for her own pleasure. I can tell she's close by the little pants she makes and how tight she keeps squeezing my dick. My erection didn't take long to come back. In fact, it's back sooner than it usually is. I use my tongue to play with her nipple until she's writhing on me and she can't stop. She drags her clit up and down my thigh.

"That's it. Come for me," I tell her. I flex my thigh and she comes undone.

Trista kisses my neck and pulls the skin into her mouth. She sucks hard, and I wouldn't be surprised if she leaves a hickey. "That's it. Good girl." She sucks my neck harder at the endearment. I say it again to see what she does, and this time she clenches around my thigh. I say it once more, and she hiccups a gasp and then sighs. I slap her ass and she curls into me.

I fist the back of her head and twist her hair until it's taut. "You keep surprising me," I say after her orgasm is over. "Good girl does it for you, huh?"

She shrugs. "I didn't know I liked it until you said it." She pauses, then says, "No one's ever called me that. It makes me tingle everywhere."

She's clinging to me like a little spider monkey. I could devour her every day and still be hungry for more. I'm already aching to be inside of her again. I've never called anyone a good girl before her, and it shockingly made my dick pulse with lust.

"Grab the condom and put it on me," I say. Trista listens and rolls it down my shaft, then she looks at me for her next step. "Get over here. I want you to ride me."

Trista straddles me. She stands on her knees and positions my cock at her entrance. She sucks in a breath, and my hands find her hips. I'm fucking straining to be inside of her.

"Go slow," she tells me. "You're the biggest guy I've ever been with. It's going to take a minute to adjust to you at this angle."

I do exactly what she asks. Trista sinks down and her back straightens. It's a deeper angle that I can feel the back of her pussy. It hurts her to take all of me like this, but she still does. Every time I thrust in, her tits press into my chest. She gives me a slow ride and we build a steady flow of friction. As our speed increases, the desire burns between us. I savor the feel of her body on mine. I grip her ass cheeks hard and dig my nails into her skin. This woman has a body to die for. How could little Timmy give this up?

I spread her cheeks apart and press a finger to her little hole. Trista rides me faster, so I push harder. Her breasts bounce in my face and her pants turn to moans. Her legs come down on the sides and she places her feet on the floor. She starts to fuck me faster, harder. She grabs a hold of the back of the chair and rides me like a horse. She mumbles to herself and pulls on my hair. She's like a little cat in heat.

"Fucking damn. You fuck me so good. Fuck me harder, Trista. Take this dick like a good girl and fuck me."

"Ahhh," she moans.

We're going to leave a wet mark on this chair from the amount of pleasure dripping between us.

"Show me how much you want my cock. Fuck me like you want me."

Trista nearly melts on me. Her pussy is soaking wet. While she may be discovering her firsts tonight, I just discovered one about myself. I like using pet names with Trista. I've never had the urge to use them in the past with other flings. But with her, something about it fills my dick with euphoria.

I wrap one arm around her hips and grip the back of her neck with my other hand. I pump into her tender pussy and fuck her hard. She bounces on my lap, begging for more. Just as she's close to the edge, I say, "Be a good girl and make me come."

And she does. We explode together in a blissful harmony, orgasming so hard we hold on to each other for dear life. I'm scared to see if the condom broke from shooting into it the way I did. I have never ordered a woman to fuck me before, or to make me come, and damn, I kind of like it.

"Fuck, Leo."

She giggles and it comes out raspy. She's damp from sweating a little that our bodies stick together. Trista moves slow once the orgasm high comes down. But I can't take my hands off her, and I already want more.

"You're going to rearrange my insides."

I chuckle this time for real. "Isn't that the goal?" She sits up and pleasure oozes from us. "Stand up for a second," I say. "I need to get this condom off."

Trista stands on wobbly legs and sits next to me. I quickly pull the condom off and reach for a new one. Walking into the other room, I throw it out and then make my way to the minibar. I grab four miniature liquor bottles and carry them to Trista.

"I think I need a little rest. I'm sore and tender right now," she says.

I shake my head and hand her two bottles.

"No rest for the wicked. Sit on my lap and face forward. Let me make you feel good."

CHAPTER SEVEN
LEO

She eyes me like I'm a lunatic. Maybe I am a little.

I sit down and face her. Twisting the cap off, I initiate a toast. We take a shot together and then do another.

"I'd offer you a cigarette, but then you'd have to go on the balcony. It's about forty-five degrees out there plus the wind chill."

"A shot will do it for me."

Sitting back, I spread my legs and roll the latex down my erection. I haven't softened.

"You're serious?" she asks me in disbelief.

"Yes. Now get over here and sit on me. I have an idea."

Surprisingly, she does as I ask.

"I thought you were going to say no."

"It's not every day a stranger rocks your world and wants to give you more of it."

My stomach tightens. I like that she wants to keep going.

I instruct her to face forward. Leaning back, I spit into my hand and rub it on her pussy. Trista guides me into her slowly like before. I can tell she's sore, so I won't rough her up too much. She sinks all the way down and then takes a deep breath. We both moan at the same time. I pull her back and direct her to lie on me with my cock inside of her. She exhales then relaxes.

"You don't have to move," I tell her. "I just want to feel you."

My fingers gently rub her clit. The softer, the better, especially after the orgasms she's had back-to-back already. I drag my fingers around and down to her entrance. Her legs are bent over mine. I slowly rock into her yet barely move. The friction makes our desires cling to each other. My finger glides along the thin skin that stretches around my cock. I palm her inner thighs and massage close to her pussy.

"I can't get enough of you," I whisper. My heart is racing in my chest. I wonder if she can feel it. "I could sit here and not move with my cock inside of you and stay hard all fucking day. That's what you do to me."

I kiss her shoulder and cup her breasts, thumbing her nipples. She clenches her thighs. I reach between our bodies again and find her clit. The way she lets me touch her spurs my need for her.

"Don't move. Just lie here and let me play with

you." She turns her head to face me, and I reach down to give her a quick kiss. "Think you can come without moving if I just rub your clit?"

"I'm willing to try," she says, her voice wistful. "I feel so full at this angle."

I kiss her neck and move painfully slow, rocking into her pussy as I rub the space between her clit and her opening, back and forth. She hisses beautifully and clenches again. Her pussy always gives her away. I shift my legs so they're over hers and tangle them in a way so they're pressed into the lounge and she can't escape. Trista is at my mercy. I drape an arm across the top of her chest and the other diagonal to stroke her clit and hold her down while I continue rocking. I kiss behind her ear and pull her lobe into my mouth. She drips down the sides of my cock the closer I get to her clit. I rub three fingers against her pussy and she moans in bliss.

"Fuck, Leo. This is torture." I notice how her teeth are pressed into her bottom lip.

"Your pussy is going to ruin me," I tell her. "I'd give anything to have a taste of you every day."

And I would. Now I understand why some men pay for sex when it feels this damn good. She lets me do what I want and enjoys it too.

"You're teasing me. Rub me faster, or I need to start fucking you. I want to come."

"I'm going to make you come like this, then you're going to bend forward and get on your knees and let me fuck you that way."

She nods. I bet I could've said I was going to take her ass and she would have agreed.

I rub her quicker, circling her clit and bringing her higher. Her pussy contracts around my cock and her legs strain against mine. I hold her hostage so she can't move. Her pants are erotic and are happening closer together. My cock fills her up, pumping into her slowly. Her hips don't move while I bring us both ecstasy.

I tease near the opening with two fingers, and she says, "Oh, Leo. Right there. Keep doing that."

She lets out small huffs of breath. Her chest rises and falls fast.

"Oh fuck, it's right here."

Trista explodes around me again. The orgasm rocks her so forcefully that she's quivering. She squirms in my hold, her breathing labored and raspy. Her pussy is relentless as it pulsates around my cock. Clear fluid seeps from her and leaks on my thighs.

"I'm glad you don't live near me," she says. "I'd want you to fuck me like this every day."

I cover her with every part of my body and hug her to me. Her bodily fluid paints my skin. The tequila must be getting to me tonight because I want to own and keep every part of Trista. Our sexual chemistry is combustive. It's so good. It's not often I find this.

"My turn," I whisper. "Except I want you to lean over the side of the bed."

She inhales deeply, and I can tell the orgasm left her exhausted.

"I'll carry you," I tell her. Given my height, the bed is the best angle for us.

I pull out of Trista and scoop her up quickly into my arms. My erection bobs between us as I walk to the bedroom. The four-poster bed is raised, so it works in my favor.

"I'm not going to be able to walk by the time we're done," she says.

"It would be the best compliment," I tell her.

I place Trista down and pinch her jaw between my finger and thumb. Tugging her chin up to mine, I thrust my tongue into her mouth and kiss her. She tangles her fingers in my hair and pulls on the strands just a little. The woman has so much passion in every kiss and touch she gives me. I lean into her, loving how she feels. I'm drowning in her. My hands slide to her soft hips. Breaking the kiss, I turn her around. She steps forward and puts one foot up on the wood bedrail. I lift her up and she climbs to her hands and knees. I watch as she boldly spreads her legs open and arches her back so her heart-shaped ass is high in the air.

"Exquisite," I tell her.

I palm one cheek and rub in circles. I'd love to spend more time playing with her body, but that would require days we don't have. I look between her legs and see her tits graze the sheets. Those babies are like giant marshmallows. My thumb brushes over her little hole and she jerks. Leaning in,

I lick her pink pussy from behind. She's tender and swollen, and still dripping with desire. I drag my tongue up her to her entrance and delve inside. I lick the cream out and slurp her up. She moans, and it urges me to continue until my cock is steel in my grip. I can't get enough of her.

Trista, like a good fucking girl, rocks into my face. Her pants grow shorter, and surprisingly, I think she's on the way to another orgasm. I thumb her clit again and lick my way up to her tiny hole. Her hips arch and she yells out. Her pussy drips like a water leak over my fingers. I feel feral and eat her ass while teasing her entrance. Her knees spread wider. I love that she hasn't hesitated at all tonight. Her orgasm comes all at once and ricochets through her body. She trembles and shakes and seizes the sheets in her fists. I wipe away some of her pleasure with my fingers and coat my cock in it. I still have the condom on from before.

"Goodness, Leo. How the hell are you making me do this?" She pounds the bottom of her fist into the bed.

"When it's good, it's fucking great."

I angle the tip at her entrance and press forward. Her hips slowly widen, and she groans deep in her throat as she takes me all the way to the hilt. We hold still, locked together, and soak in the blissful pleasure swimming between us. I rock into Trista and inhale through my nostrils, trying not to orgasm. The warmth of her body and touch of her skin makes me crazy with hunger. I want to dominate every part of her.

"I didn't think it was possible to be worn out from sex," Trista says with her face smushed into the bed. "My legs feel like Jell-O."

I pump into her with the need to claim her as mine. I fight against the compulsion and let the thoughts go since I can't do that despite how much I want to. An orgasm swirls in my balls, and my fingers dig into her hips. I don't know if it's the alcohol tonight or what that is making me crazy for Trista. I've had drunker one-night stands in the past and never felt this compelled.

Trista notices a change in my pace. She spreads her knees wider and opens herself to me. I sink into her pussy and exhale a long breath of bliss.

"You won't be able to leave my bed after this," I say.

My hips piston against hers as my orgasm zips up my spine and explodes into the condom. I almost fall forward from the force of pleasure whipping through me. I climax in waves and she takes the brunt of the impact.

"If you want to have any more of me, you'll give me a break."

I nod even though she can't see it. I'm panting as I pull out and slide next to her body. A body should be cherished.

Wrapping an arm around her waist, I pull her down so she collapses on me. Surprisingly, I need a break too. I'm feeling tired and want to fall asleep with Trista.

I tear the condom off in one swoop and toss it to the side on the floor. I'll take care of it tomorrow. Turning over, I cover Trista like a blanket and look down into her sleepy eyes.

I brush the hair away from her face. "I'm glad you walked into the bar tonight," I tell her.

"Me too," she says softly. "Thanks for being my first official one-night stand."

I kiss her forehead. She blinks slowly then drifts off to sleep in my arms.

I reach between us and push my fingers against her clit. She moves against me in her sleep and lifts her leg up to rest over mine. She sighs as my fingers delve further between her legs and caress her pussy. I watch her eyelids to see if she's awake, but she's not. It's been a fantasy of mine to pleasure my girlfriend while she's sleeping. I want to see if I can make her orgasm. Trista may not be my girlfriend, but she is for the night.

The tip of my cock rubs against her belly. I stroke her clit, feeling her tender folds and plump pussy lips. She drips between my fingers. Gently, I roll her onto her back and take one of her large nipples into my mouth. I suckle it, and she doesn't move as I drag my cock up and down her side, wishing it was in her. I love that she's mine to play with. I tease her pussy, playfully touching her and manipulating her lips. I insert a finger then pull out and drag it up to her clit. Her body jerks, so I do it again. She wants me even in her sleep. Crawling on top of Trista, I press her breasts together and smush my face between them as my cock drags along her clit. I flick my tongue over both nipples and pull on them until they're hard.

I reach for the last condom and roll it on. Her hips begin to move and her legs scissor against mine. I can tell she's horny.

I settle between her legs and spread her knees wide. I'm addicted to her pussy and need her again. I could stay munching on her every night with how good she tastes. Her clit sticks out between her pussy lips, and I play with it, loving how slippery she is.

Gripping my cock, I press the tip inside and slowly surge in all the way.

Fuck. I groan inwardly. Her tight warmth feels like home.

My balls drag on the bed while I slow fuck Trista in her sleep.

CHAPTER EIGHT
TRISTA

There's a knock on the door that rouses me.

I roll over and clench my eyes shut from the sunrays shining between the curtains. I take in my surroundings, and everything comes rushing back to me.

Uncle Joe's. Leo. Tim. Tequila. Orgasms. Many, many orgasms.

Leo mumbles as he stirs behind me and gets out of bed. I turn over and watch him walk naked toward a chair by the window. My tender clit throbs at the sight of him. I still don't know how old he is, but after last night, I'd say he has the stamina of a twenty-year-old.

Leo swipes a robe off the chair and quickly slips it on as he heads out of the room. I curl on my side and have a full view of the living room area. Moments later, room service strolls across my field of vision pushing a cart. Leo directs the server to place two dome-covered plates, a carafe of coffee, and a glass container of what looks like milk on the coffee table. The server lifts the stainless-steel lids, revealing a plate of fresh-cut fruit in different shapes and a plate filled with pastries. Room service leaves, and Leo returns to the bedroom. He rubs his eyes with the heel of his hands.

"I forgot I had room service set up in advance. Sorry about waking you," Leo says apologetically.

His groggy voice is cute. I shake my head and give him a lazy smile. "Nothing is better than being woken up with fresh coffee."

I inhale deeply and let out a sigh. I bet the coffee at this hotel is actually good.

Leo eyes me quietly, insinuation heavy in his gaze. "I can think of something," he says and unties his belt. He pulls back the lapels and the robe falls in a heap on the floor. Lord have mercy, he's gorgeous in the light.

"You're kidding me. You just opened your eyes ten seconds ago."

"And I'm already hungry for you."

Leo grabs his erection and strokes it before bending one knee to the mattress and climbing onto the bed. He has a nice body, toned and muscular, and not like he spends his Sundays at the gym for fun. He swipes the sheet away, exposing me. I'm still floating from last night, and my body comes alive. My knees snap shut, and I giggle as he tries to pry them open.

"This is how I planned to wake you up," Leo says once he gets what he wants. He flattens his tongue and licks a wet trail from the bottom of my pussy to my clit, where he suctions his mouth and draws on me like I'm the sweetest nectar he's ever tasted. My hips undulate into him and I take the pleasure he's giving me. Leo was right. He's going to have me comparing every guy I have sex with to him after this. Tim didn't love to go down on me the way Leo does.

I feel bad comparing Tim to Leo. I was happy with what Tim did to me in the bedroom. I didn't have too many complaints.

But this is just so much better. I can't go back to what I had, and I won't. Not after what I've experienced and tasted. My hips widen and I press Leo's face against my pussy. It's ironic how Tim is the one who wanted to explore yet I'm the one who struck gold with Leo.

"You're so good at this," I say in between pants, moaning in bliss.

I let go of my reservations at some point last night and submitted myself to him. My inhibitions departed from my body, and I was okay with it.

"I like knowing I'm the best," he says against my pussy.

Leo pulls back and sits on his knees. He strokes the top of his cock down my pussy then coats himself in my pleasure.

"I don't have any more condoms left," he says.

I blink. "We used them all?"

"I have a confession to make," he says, staring down at me.

My brows rise. "What could you have done?" I reach for his cock and slowly stroke his erection. He's so hard, and it surprises me a little after the number of times he orgasmed last night.

"When you fell asleep, I had every intention of doing the same next to you. You looked so beautiful and peaceful sprawled out that I needed you one more time."

My eyes widen. I stop stroking him, but I don't let go. I tighten my grip. "You fucked me while I was sleeping?" I ask, a little stunned.

He nods. "I've never done that before. I feel a little guilty about it."

I frown. My gaze falls to the tip of his cock, and I watch a creamy dollop drop to the bed. "How didn't I wake up?"

"I went slow. I didn't hurt you. I wasn't forceful. I just wanted to feel you." He pauses, sucking in a breath as I twist my grip down his shaft. "I'm not a creeper who forces themselves on women. After the things we did, I feel like you and I are different, and you wouldn't have opposed it."

I glance back up to his eyes, internalizing how I feel. I'm not in any pain whatsoever, and if he hadn't told me, I never would have known. I'm oddly appreciative that he did tell me.

While I'll never admit it out loud, a deep, dark part of me is turned on by what he did. Leo is sort of a wicked wet dream.

"Did I like it?" I ask curiously.

He nods and shuffles forward on his knees. "You

made little sounds in your sleep. Your legs moved when I played with your clit. You were wet and slippery when I slid in and out."

I swallow thickly. My clit zings at the mention of it, and wetness coats my pussy.

"I won't have sex without a condom. But I can do other things if you want."

Leo leans over me. His biceps form a cage around my head. He lays his hips on top of mine. My teeth dig into my bottom lip at the touch of his cock straining against my pussy. I moan, and he sees that I like what he's doing.

"I definitely want," Leo growls, then surges against me. "You're irresistible."

A blush crawls up my chest. He bends down and kisses me. He presses hard and thrusts his tongue into my mouth. I take it and tangle mine around his.

"You're going to be so hard to walk away from," he says when he breaks the kiss.

His words pinch my heart.

I grab the back of his hips and grind him against my clit. Damn, it feels good. Wetness slips from me and slides against his cock. His hips pump against mine as he glides his cock up and down my pussy. Leo doesn't hide how hungry he is for me and that does something to me. It makes me realize that I always want to feel this way. Drawing him in, I kiss him back with the same passionate intensity he's giving me.

His hand falls to my throat and he applies pressure at the same time he gyrates against my clit.

I gasp, and my back bows at the pleasure. Leo dips down and takes a nipple into his mouth. He bites and tugs and sucks hard until I'm writhing under him.

"I bet I could make you come like this. Just with my mouth on your nipple and nothing else."

A raspy giggle escapes me. I've never orgasmed from my nipples being played with alone, and now I'm curious if it's possible. "If you want to give it a shot, I'm game."

"Put your arms above your head and leave them there. Keep your eyes closed and think about what I'm doing to you," he says, and I follow his instructions.

Leo pulls his hips back and a cool breeze blows against my pussy. I mope for a split second before his lips find my nipple. He flattens his tongue and licks and laps. He pinches the other one before gripping it. Leo creates a steady game of lust. There's a bite of forcefulness with him, and I like that.

His breath is hot against my breast. He runs his mouth around my nipple. The dark stubble on his chin heightens the pleasure and sends it steamrolling through my blood. The little hairs prickle my sensitive skin and it feels oddly good. He uses them to tease me. I clench my thighs together, needing my clit to be touched, and my chest rises against his face. His tongue flicks fast over my nipple. An orgasm starts at the base of my spine and I sigh. I wiggle against Leo, chasing the pleasure.

"Fuck. I want you to fuck me. You're killing me with this," I admit.

Leo bites my nipple between his teeth and pulls it back until I'm gasping. He let's go and it burns for a split second.

"My cock is so fucking hard for you right now," he says. "I want to fill you up with it." I'm panting as he licks, surprised by the pleasure. "You want me to fuck you?" he asks.

I squeeze my eyes shut, fighting against opening them. My body says yes, but my brain says no. Leo twists just the tip of my other nipple and it causes a zing in my clit.

"Yes," I whisper.

He growls. "If I fuck you without a condom, then I'm going to come inside your pussy. I don't pull out, and I definitely won't be able to once I'm inside you. My cum will be dripping out of you for days."

My pussy is already dripping. Why does that sound so damn hot? My mind is running with fantasies of white fluid seeping out of me.

Who am I, and what did Leo do with Trista?

"I want to feel you come inside of me," I tell him.

"You're going to be covered in my cum when I'm done. I'm not going to fuck you hard and fast. It's going to be a slow goodbye ride, where I enjoy every last bit of you. I'm going to make you soak the sheets."

A heart-pounding orgasm washes over me at the

thought. I come as he plays with only my nipples and breasts. A loud gush of air explodes from my lungs. My clit is still throbbing, but pleasure runs down my spine and leaves me tingling for more.

"Open your legs," he demands, and I spread them fast.

Leo slaps his cock against my pussy, and it's like a piece of steel. He drags the tip up and down and presses it against my entrance. My hips curl up to give him access to slide into me. Either I'm still tipsy from last night or he has the ability to make me change my mind with mind-blowing orgasms. I've experienced and discovered a few things about myself since meeting Leo that will leave me questioning things for days to come.

Leo brushes the hair back from my forehead. "I assume by you asking for this that you're clean?"

I nod my head, knowing what he's talking about. "I'm tested when I get my yearly checkup."

"The food industry tests too. I always use protection," he says, and pauses. "Like I said earlier, you're just different."

I pull him down to about an inch from my face. "So are you," I say.

Leo reaches between us and guides his bare cock into my pussy. The veins in his arms pulse as I watch him disappear inside of me.

I suck in a breath. The intimacy of being skin to skin like this awakens a desire in me. I kiss his shoulder and welcome him into my body. Leo surges back, then slides all the way in until he can't get any deeper and pumps against my clit. He holds me tight, kissing my lips until I'm breathless. He's all over me, consuming me, fucking my body like it's his job to make me feel like I'm high on orgasms. The passion we create is ecstasy to my blood.

Leo sits back on his knees and takes me with him. I straddle his thighs. The sheets are crumpled and messy around us. He grips my hips and pushes me down on his cock. I feel every ridge of him and wonder how I can ever use a condom after this. My hips arch as I sink down and take every inch of this stranger who's changed me. Leo wraps his arms around my lower back then places his face between my breasts and rubs me on him. He pumps into me, and I greedily take him because I need his cock. I want it.

Sadly, my mind flashes to Tim, and I think about how I never had this chemistry with him.

I can tell by the way Leo has sex that he's a lover who puts all the time in. Our movements are slow as Leo barely pulls out. He thrusts back all the way inside, and I gasp. Delicious pressure builds between us. He holds me close, the way I imagine two lovers would when they're making real love, and takes us to the edge. I'm soaking wet and sticky from the both of us.

"I won't be able to hold on much longer," I tell him. Little beads of sweat bubble on the back of my neck. "Please, I want to come with you."

CHAPTER NINE
TRISTA

Leo bites the curve of my neck.

"The moment you start to come is when I will. I won't be able to hold it off when your pussy starts contracting. I can't get enough of how your pussy sucks my dick."

A couple more delicious pumps, then Leo is kissing me deeply and we're coming together. His cock juts inside me, jerking against my walls as he unloads his cum. I rock into him, and his orgasm carries me higher.

We slow down. Our kisses slow too. The only sound in the room is our heavy breathing. I try to get off, but he doesn't let me. Leo holds me tighter to him and kisses me like he's thanking me. He rises up on his knees and cradles me to the bed. His cock is naturally thick and feels full inside of me. He pulls back and slowly thrusts inside before he pulls out and kisses his way down my body to my pussy. Leo spreads my knees back, and his eyes grow heavy at what he sees. He presses a finger to my entrance and moves his cum around my pussy. Goose bumps break out down my arms.

"Like what you see?" I ask. His Adam's apple bobs.

"Very much. If I didn't have a flight to catch, I'd say you have to stay like this all day so I can look at you whenever I want. Do you want to shower before you leave?"

"I think I'd rather wear you home," I tell him.

His eyes flash to mine, and I swear I hear a growl in his chest. "It's a good thing we're an ocean apart," he says, climbing off the bed. Leo steps into a pair of boxers and pulls them up. He tucks his cock away while standing in front of me as if he's done it a hundred times.

"Why's that?" I ask and pull the sheet up my chest. I feel like I don't have a care in the world after all the orgasms I've had. Any stress I built up or unworthiness I felt is gone. Who knew all it took was some good dick to whip my ass back into shape.

"Because I wouldn't let you leave my bed. I'd get nothing done."

I blush. "I take that as a compliment."

Leo walks out to the living room, then returns with two mugs filled with steaming coffee. I sit up when he hands me one. "Are you still going to say coffee is better to wake up to than sex?"

I give him an amusing stare. A giddiness takes over me and I can't stop smiling. "Your sex is on another level. You can't compare that to coffee. I'm going to be in a daze for the rest of the day. What time do you have to leave?" I ask, cupping the warm mug.

"In about an hour. I PreCheck, so it doesn't take me long."

"What am I supposed to wear back to my place?" I ask. I'm talking to Leo like I've known him my whole life. "Actually, I could text Noelle and have her bring me clothes."

It dawns on me that I never sent her my location last night. I hope she isn't worried about me.

Leo bends down and shuffles around in his luggage. He picks up a pair of sweatpants and a matching hoodie then tosses them to me. I hold up the double extra-large sweater and read the front.

"You went to Stanford?" I ask, and he nods. "I can't take this."

"Take it. I have plenty of them." Leo walks away before I can protest. He returns in a flash holding something in his hand. "The hotel gives everyone complimentary white flip-flops. You can wear these out instead of your high heels."

My eyes light up. "Thanks. That's thoughtful of you. Now the walk of shame won't be nearly as bad."

He chuckles then gives me a pointed stare like something dawned on him. "I can give you a laundry bag for your shoes so no one sees what you're carrying."

"You're the ideal one-night stand partner. Now you're going above and beyond."

"I have this room until two. You can stay and order food, then I'll have my driver take you home."

I consider the idea since I have nothing else to do, but I should probably get going. I get out of bed and dress in the sweatpants and hoodie he gave me. I fluff out my hair and curse myself for not carrying a hair tie. Leo eyes my body like he wants to take a bite out of it again. I like the way he looks at me.

"Come eat," he says, but it comes out more like a demand.

I follow him like a lost kitten to the coffee table in the living room. My jaw drops at the assortment of food.

"Wow. These aren't from the hotel, are they?"

Leo hands me a ceramic plate then takes one for himself. "No. When I come to Chicago, I always have Sugar Moon Bakery. Have you been?"

I shake my head, in awe of the food. I want to try one of everything. "No, I haven't actually."

Leo begins cutting the scones into pieces. There are savory and sweet options. He places a bit of each on my plate as if he read my mind.

"My hero," I say, and Leo smiles. I like the way it looks on him. "When will you be back in the city?"

I use the mini tongs to pick up kiwi in the shape of the sun.

"It really depends on what my client needs. I'll definitely be here for the opening, but before that, I'm not sure."

I follow Leo to the table near the balcony with a

view of the city and take a seat. He retrieves our mugs and then brings over the carafe to refill my coffee.

"Thank you," I say.

I try to recall if Tim ever refilled my cup without having to be asked. Unless it was wine, he didn't do it. I glance at the wintery skyline and take in the foggy view.

"How old are you?" I ask.

His eyes glisten in the morning light. "I'm about ten years older than I look." He pauses. "I'm fifty-seven."

Holy shit. I quickly do the math in my head. He's thirty-three years older than me.

I fucked a grandpa.

But he definitely doesn't fuck like one.

Noelle is going to have a field day with me.

"You're quiet."

I glance down at my plate and try to find the words. "I just wasn't expecting that. I thought you were maybe in your forties. Not pushing sixty."

Leo let's out a laugh. No wonder he knows how to make a woman orgasm so hard. He's had a lot of practice.

"Does it bother you?" he asks.

Pursing my lips together, I shake my head. "Does it bother you that I'm twenty-four?"

"You know it doesn't. I could tell when you walked into the bar you were young."

I shouldn't ask, but I can't help it. "Do you normally go for younger women?"

"I don't have an age preference. Like I told you last night, age is just a number."

I raise my coffee mug to him. "Do you have kids?" I ask.

"None that I know of."

This time I laugh. We make idle small talk for the next twenty minutes. I clean up our plates and coffee. Leo steps into his jeans and pockets his wallet but not before sliding out a business card. He passes it to me. I glance down and read it.

"Maybe I'll see you again when I'm back. You can save my number in your phone."

I flip the card back and forth between my fingers, debating if I want to take it. I read over his name and occupation. I bite the side of my lip before I hand it back to him.

"Let's see if we run into each other again," I say, taking him back to last night and the words he said. "I'll be working down there until mid-January." I tilt my head toward the window, indicating downtown.

"What will you do after that?" he asks.

I shrug, grabbing the laundry tote. I stuff my high heels into the bag. "I'm a freelancer, so I can work anywhere. I don't have another project set up at the moment, but I'm not worried. I'll find something. I can travel if I need to. I have an apartment in the city."

"Do you work out of state?"

"Sometimes I work in Los Angeles or New York."

Leo picks up the dress he tore from my body. "I'll replace it and find a way to get it to you."

I shake my head. "The dress was old and too tight anyway. I don't need it replaced."

I take the torn fabric and dump it in the trash. Looking around, I make sure I have everything I need. Leo takes his luggage by the handle.

"I'll have my driver take you home," he says as we walk toward the door.

"Don't worry about it. I'm going to text my friend and will probably take the bus to see her."

Leo wheels his luggage out, and I pick up my purse. We take the elevator down to the lobby and stride through the double doors to the sidewalk. Cool air billows against my cheeks. Snow and the scent of balsam fir fill the air.

"Thanks for last night," I say, then instantly regret it. "Do people say that after one-night stands?"

Leo gives me an amusing smirk. "Not usually." He pauses, then says to my surprise, "I hope I run into you again."

I beam up at him like a happy little girl. I wrap my arms around his shoulders and press a kiss to his mouth. I'm standing on my tiptoes when he lifts me up and kisses me back. His fingers thread through the hair at the back of my head. He fists my locks and kisses me goodbye. It stings a bit that he's leaving. Leo and I hit it off. If he wasn't here on business, I think there could have been more to us than just one night.

85

His car arrives, and Leo lowers me to my feet. It's the same Land Rover from last night.

"People don't do that after a one-night stand either," he mumbles against my lips.

His luggage is placed in the trunk, and the driver opens the rear door for him.

"Have a good flight," I say.

Leo gets in the car and the door shuts. I had a good time with him. He was the perfect rebound.

The Land Rover pulls away, and I walk back inside the warm lobby to text Noelle. I ask if she wants to meet for mimosas. I need to fill her in on last night with my irresistible stranger. She tells me her car is in the shop but that she'll take the bus to see me. We'll meet in twenty minutes. I ask her to bring me a pair of socks and sneakers to borrow. My toes are cold, and I don't want to drink in flip-flops. The last time I did that, I lost them.

As I go to put my cell phone away, I get a text message from Tim.

My stomach drops. I hover above the notification. Yesterday, I would have opened the message.

I click the side button to lock my screen before slipping my phone into my purse. I decide that I'm not going to look at it. Things are different now.

I'm different.

Tim didn't want me anymore. Now he can't have me.

Maybe Leo was right. Maybe I did need a good one-night stand. I feel rejuvenated and like a completely different person. There's a pep in my step. I have clarity and self-worth that I didn't have before. And to think I got that from a sexy stranger who nearly blew my back out.

I leave the hotel and set out to meet Noelle. She's going to eat this up and never let me live it down. I can't wait to tell her.

The hoodie I'm wearing smells like him. Because of this, now I don't know if I can wash it.

I'm feeling sentimental. I bet that doesn't usually happen with one-night stands either.

A smile fills my face.

I hope I run into Leo again someday.

The End.

About Lucia

Lucia Franco resides in South Florida with her husband and two sons. She was a competitive athlete for over ten years–a gymnast and cheerleader–which heavily inspired the Off Balance series.

Her novel Hush, Hush was a finalist in the 2019 Stiletto Contest hosted by Contemporary Romance Writers, a chapter of Romance Writers of America. Her novels are being translated into several languages.

She's written more than a dozen books and can be found rambling on Instagram.

Find out more at authorluciafranco.com.

Made in the USA
Monee, IL
06 December 2024

72761889R10056